FIGHTER

Leslie McGill

SADDLEBACK
EDUCATIONAL PUBLISHING

CAP CENTRAL

Fighter
Running Scared
Hacker
Gearhead
The Game
Hero

EDUCATIONAL PUBLISHING
www.sdlback.com

ISBN-13: 978-1-62250-705-4
ISBN-10: 1-62250-705-3
eBook: 978-1-61247-956-9

Printed in Guangzhou, China
NOR/0715/CA21501087

19 18 17 16 15   3 4 5 6 7

To David, who never lost faith in me.

CHAPTER 1

JAIR

Jair Nobles woke up with a jolt. It felt like the day before Christmas. For a moment he wondered why he felt so excited. Then he remembered. Last night he chatted on the computer with Keisha Jackson. Keisha was beautiful: light brown eyes, coppery smooth skin, and long dreads. She wore clothes that showed as much as she could while still following Capital Central High School's dress code.

Keisha was one of the most popular students at the school. She had just been elected president of the student government association. She hung out with Eva Morales, Joss White, and that whole in-crowd. Kids who never paid any attention to him. There was nothing she said that made it look like she liked him, but at least she chatted with him. It was enough to give him hope.

He got out of bed, trying not to wake Royce and Marcel, his two younger brothers. He tiptoed into the living room. His mom's computer sat on a table. The table was missing a leg. His mother had propped it up with cinder blocks. The cinder block side was higher than the others, so the table wobbled every time he hit a key.

He retrieved the chat from the night before. He looked over everything he and Keisha had talked about: Mrs. Lewis's exam next week on the three branches of government, the upcoming field trip to the US Supreme Court, and people at school. She had even asked for his advice. As student government president, she had to choose an issue for the students to focus on during the year. Two years ago, the subject was tolerance toward students new to the US. Last year, it was tolerance for gay students. Keisha didn't know of any other groups that Cap Cent kids needed to be tolerant of, so she had asked Jair what he thought. He hadn't been able to think of a topic. But he was flattered she had asked his opinion.

He went back into his room to get dressed. He rummaged through the broken laundry basket on the floor to find a clean shirt. Nothing. A few pairs of his brothers' tighty-whities but none of his boxers and no shirts. He picked up a T-shirt from the floor and smelled it. He made a face and threw it down.

Jair couldn't remember when his mother had last washed clothes. Or made them a real meal. He was glad she'd finally found a job. She had been looking for such a long time. He hoped that her salary would soon start to help make up for all they lost when his dad was laid off from the post office. But her new job kept her away from home for the whole day. The doctors she worked for kept their office open for long hours. They needed to hire more office staff. His mother spent the day answering phones and dealing with angry patients who had been on hold too long. She was so tired when she got home. She didn't have energy to do anything. And his dad was useless.

He opened his closet and found a shirt that he sometimes wore to church. It was one of his best. He never wore it to school. But now that

Keisha had finally noticed him, he wanted to look good.

Jair picked up his blue Washington Wizards cap. He carefully placed it on his head. If he kept the back strap fairly tight, the cap sat up higher, making him look taller. He hated being so short. Back in middle school, he'd figured he just hadn't started growing yet. But now that he was in high school, it was looking more and more like he'd inherited his mother's shortness instead of his father's height. Most of the other boys in high school were taller than he was. He figured they were all secretly laughing at him for being short. He knew that was how he would feel if he were tall and was looking at a guy who was no bigger than a seventh grader.

He went into the kitchen and opened the refrigerator to find something to eat. He sniffed the open carton of milk. The smell made him cringe. Spoiled. So no cereal unless he ate it dry. Looked like he'd have to eat both breakfast and lunch at school. Again.

He started for the door. "Jair? Baby, is that you?" his mother's sleepy voice called from the bedroom.

He turned. "Mom? Don't you need to get up?" he asked.

"I'm going to," she said sleepily. "Get your brothers up and make sure they get dressed," she added. "I'm just not up to it today."

Jair had wanted to get to school early to try and hang out with Keisha. "Mom, I have something I gotta do," he said. "Can't you do it?"

"Boy, you disrespecting your mother?"

At the sound of his father's voice, Jair felt his usual mix of fear and anger. He hadn't realized his father was home. Since he lost his job, it seemed like he was never around. Which was fine with Jair. Fewer nights with his father in the apartment meant fewer chances of getting in trouble for something he did or had forgotten to do. When his father was home, he often had visitors—rough-looking guys who Jair didn't know. None of them stayed very long. Jair stayed in his room when they came around because they made him uncomfortable.

Jair had no idea what his father did when he wasn't at their apartment. All he knew was that when his father showed up, he brought trouble with him. It seemed like he was drinking more too. And when he drank, the slightest little thing would set him off. Not a week went by that his father didn't hit one of them.

"No, sir," Jair said. "I'll get them up."

"And watch your tone," his father said.

"Yes, sir," Jair said automatically as he walked back to his bedroom.

He gave Royce a hard shove, then shoved Marcel.

"Hey!" they both protested.

"Get up, you losers," he said meanly. "I need to get to school, and Mom said you need to get going."

Neither of the younger boys made a move. Jair went to Royce—the middle brother—and pulled him out of bed, dropping him roughly on the floor.

Royce scrambled to get away. "Mom!" he wailed.

"Boys, don't make me come in there!" their father yelled from the other room. "Next time you have to be told, it will be my belt does the talking!"

"Get up!" Jair hissed to Royce. "I want to get out of here."

Royce headed for the bathroom.

"Jair's got a girlfriend! Jair's got a girlfriend!" Marcel sang from under his covers. "Jair's so stupid, he left the computer on for everyone to see!"

Jair was furious. "You shut up, you little punk!" he yelled. He began hitting his youngest brother as hard as he could through the bedcovers.

"Dad! Jair's hitting me!" Marcel yelled.

Jair felt himself being picked up. His father threw him against the bedroom wall with such force that he was dazed for a moment.

"You think you're a tough guy? Picking on a little kid?" his father said coldly. "You ain't so tough. You ain't no bigger than a girl. And don't you be cryin' neither. There are no girls in this family."

Jair bit his lip to keep his father from seeing how his words hurt. His stomach heaved with a mixture of hurt feelings and hatred. Bad enough that the other guys at school disrespected him for being so short. He had tried to make up for it by being one of the meanest, toughest kids in school. But he couldn't do that with his father.

"Now get out of here before I beat your ass again," his father said, walking out of the room.

Jair shook himself off and headed for the door. Even if he didn't see Keisha, being at school would be better than being at home.

CHAPTER 2

ZANDER

Zander Peterson scowled at his reflection. He wasn't ready for this. Five different schools in six years. Always the new kid. Forget having a girlfriend. He'd never stayed in one place long enough to make any friends at all.

No wonder he always got into fights. All those counselors he had to talk to tried to come up with complicated reasons for the fighting.

"A reaction to his mother's absence."

"Trying to live up to his father's image."

Or the catch-all, "He has anger issues."

No one would listen when he told the truth: new kids get picked on. And he'd rather punch than get punched. Simple as that. Sure, it was hard trying to deal with his mother's long deployment to Afghanistan. And having an air force colonel for a father could be hard at times. But Zander knew he didn't need counseling. His issues weren't anger issues—they were payback. Simple cause and effect. *Pick on me, you get punched. Any questions?*

He showered quickly. As he dried off, he thought about what to wear for his first day. The moving van had unloaded their stuff on Saturday. He'd spent Sunday setting up his PlayStation and TV. He hadn't gotten around to unpacking the boxes of clothes yet. He dug through the suitcase he'd brought with him on the plane from Los Angeles. He had no idea how kids dressed in Washington, D.C. He'd learned the hard way that kids dressed differently in different cities.

He pulled out a bright aqua T-shirt, aqua-and-purple plaid shirt, and dark purple cordu-roy slacks. He packed his lunch and made sure his transfer papers were in his backpack.

At least he no longer had to come in with his parents. He'd started enough new schools to know the process. As soon as they got word they were moving to Washington, D.C., his father checked out the city's schools. He found them an apartment near Capital Central High School, in the northeast quadrant of the city. He had the school send out all the enrollment documents so he could sign them ahead of time.

"With this new job," Colonel Peterson said, "you're going to have to be on your own more than you're used to. Can I count on you to handle that responsibility?"

I always have, Zander thought to himself. "Yes, sir," he answered in the manner his father insisted upon.

"I know moving has been hard for you, but sometimes life doesn't happen like you want," his father added.

Ya think? he thought sarcastically. "Yes, sir," he said.

Zander walked up Fifteenth Street to Bladensburg Road, and then turned on K Street toward the school. He'd seen the school Saturday night. He and his father had driven past it on their way to find a place to eat dinner. The school was big, which made sense since the Internet said close to twenty-five hundred kids went there. The football field was in good shape, and the basketball hoops had all their nets. His last school in L.A. was a wreck. He was glad that his dad got transferred out of there quickly. The Texas school before that also needed work. At least on looks, this one was the best so far.

Zander opened the front door of the school and walked into the main office.

"Hi, I'm new," he said to the pleasant-looking woman behind the high counter. He extended his hand. "Zander Peterson."

"Well, hello, Zander. Welcome," the woman said with a friendly smile as she shook his hand. "I'm Mrs. Dominguez, Mrs. Hess's secretary. Mrs. Hess is our principal," she explained. "Do you have some paperwork for me?"

Zander reached into his backpack and pulled out the envelope containing all the documents. Mrs. Dominguez shuffled through them quickly.

"Oh, these are just the signed papers," she said. "We got your class list from your old school, but we never received your permanent file. I'll have to get that from them. But no problem, we can take care of that later."

Zander nearly laughed at the thought of the school's reaction when his thick file arrived. Mrs.

Dominguez might not be so friendly when she saw the number of times he'd been suspended for fighting.

"Here is your schedule," Mrs. Dominguez said. "You have four ninety-minute classes on even days and four on odd days. First period just started, and it looks like you have—" she adjusted her glasses on the end of her nose. "Okay, yes, you have Spanish with Mr. Guevara. It's in room two fourteen. That's up the first stairway, turn right, go down to the next corridor, turn left, and there you are. Think you can find it?"

"I'll be fine," Zander said, turning for the door. "Thanks."

He remembered the "up the first stairway" part but forgot the rest. After a series of wrong turns, he finally found room 214. The door was open, so he walked in.

"You must be Zander Peterson," Mr. Guevara said, looking at a form on his desk. "Welcome. There's an empty seat over by the window."

The class was quiet as he walked across the room and sat down in the empty desk. He felt like every pair of eyes was focused on him. He stuck his backpack under his desk. This was always the hard part. Knowing that everyone was looking at you.

"Hey," the kid in the desk in front of him said, turning around. "I'm Ferg. Ferg Ferguson."

The kid took up the whole seat and spilled out over the sides. He wasn't fat, just big. But he had a friendly smile on his face. "Lionel, actually," he said with a grin. "But everyone calls me Ferg."

Zander stuck out his fist for a bump. "Zander," he answered. "How's this class?"

"*No está mal*," the girl sitting beside Zander answered. "I'm Eva, by the way. How's your Spanish?"

"*Sé un poco*," he said. He had learned a little Spanish while living a short time in Los Angeles.

"Zander, we're working on a warm-up right now," Mr. Guevara said. "Eva and Ferg, maybe you could show Zander what he needs to do and help him keep up."

"I can do it, *señor Guevara*," a pretty girl sitting behind Eva said. "*Sería mi placer.*" She leaned forward. "Hi! I'm Keisha," she added.

"*Gracias, señorita Jackson,*" Mr. Guevara answered.

"Here," the girl said. "You can share my book until you get one of your own." She moved her desk up so that it was beside Zander's.

Zander felt like his brain had shut down. Keisha was beautiful. Her hair was in dreads that she had pulled back in an elastic band. Her brown eyes were huge, framed by thick eyelashes. He couldn't believe that such a pretty girl would be so friendly. She handed him a piece of notebook paper and told him how the warm-up exercise worked.

"So why are you here?" Eva whispered.

"My parents are in the military," Zander answered. "We move around a lot."

"Pentagon?" Keisha asked.

"Yeah, and Afghanistan, actually," Zander said. It always hurt to say the word. He was always worried about his mother. Although she was a medic and not in combat, she was still in danger.

"Sorry," Eva said. "Hey, let's see your schedule," she whispered.

Zander fished in his backpack. He brought out his schedule card and handed it to her. "I am totally lost," he said, shaking his head. "This place is huge!"

"You'll figure it out soon enough," Eva said, looking at the schedule. "Okay, you have NSL with Mrs. Lewis next period. That's upstairs on the third floor."

"Oh!" Keisha said happily. "I'm in that class. I can walk with you," she added.

"That'd be great," Zander said. "But what is it?"

Keisha giggled. "National, state, and local government," she said. "We just call it NSL."

"Uh, Zander, let me give you a word of advice," Mr. Guevara said. "I am sorry that the only empty desk was beside the biggest talker in the class. But do yourself a favor and ignore Eva when she tries to get your life story, okay?"

"Hey, not fair!" Eva said in mock anger. "It was Keisha who was talking!"

"Girl—" Keisha started.

"I don't care who it was. Just quit talking. And don't get the new kid in trouble," Mr. Guevara warned.

After what seemed like forever, the bell rang, and everyone packed up their work. Zander waited until Keisha was ready, and he walked with her out of the classroom. Ferg and Eva were still in the hall and had been joined by another girl.

"This is Joss," Eva said.

"Hi!" the girl answered. "I heard we got a newbie today. Welcome!"

"News travels fast around here, huh?" Zander said with a laugh.

"Well, you don't look like a typical Cap Cent kid, so there's a buzz. Where are you from?" Joss asked.

"L.A.," Zander said. "Got here this weekend."

"Well, that explains a lot!" Eva laughed.

"What does it explain?" Zander asked.

"Duh. Your clothes!" Eva said, shaking her head. "No one in D.C. dresses like they just walked out of a magazine."

Zander looked down at his clothes and then looked at the other students passing by. Most were wearing black clothes or at least dark colors. His brightly colored clothes stuck out like they were lit by a spotlight.

"What's wrong with the way I'm dressed?" he asked.

"Nothing! You're actually giving the place some class," Joss said.

"Hey, I've got class!" Ferg said in a hurt voice.

"Right." Eva laughed as they all started down the hall. "Ferg, you wouldn't wear shoes like that if you were on the red carpet." She pointed to Zander's suede desert boots. "All the guys here ever wear are athletic shoes," she explained.

Zander looked at the feet of the other guys. It was true—they were all wearing sneakers.

"And your clothes are ... more colorful," she continued.

"Eva, leave him alone!" Keisha laughed. "Enough with the fashion talk. Our class is around the corner," she announced to Zander. "Ignore Eva. She has no filter. Any thought that pops into her head comes out her mouth!"

"No problem," Zander said. He didn't mind. They all seemed pretty friendly. "So what's this class like?" he asked Keisha as they arrived at the door.

"Boring on the good days, deadly on the bad," Keisha said.

Zander wished they didn't have to go into the room. He wanted to talk to Keisha longer. She was one of the prettiest girls he had ever seen.

"That good, huh?" he said.

"Mrs. Lewis can make math look fascinating. Since she teaches government," Keisha said.

Zander laughed as he followed Keisha into the classroom. "I guess this'll be nap time, then," he said.

Keisha laughed hard. "True that," she said. "Mrs. Lewis, this is Zander Peterson," she announced, stopping by the teacher's desk. "He's new."

"Hey, Keisha, who's the new girl?" a voice called out from the back of the room.

Keisha whirled around. "Jair!" Keisha said in a shocked voice.

Zander felt all eyes on him, watching to see if he would react. The skin on the back of his neck burned. He clenched his fist, then focused on his breathing as he'd been taught.

Walking over to the teacher, he said, "Hi. I'm Zander."

"Zander, welcome," the teacher said. "There's an empty desk back in the corner."

Zander walked back to the empty desk. He looked at the other students as he passed. Most looked at him curiously. But one kid stared at him with a smirk. He would put money on this being Jair. He kept looking at the kid as he walked down the aisle toward the empty desk. He wouldn't give the guy the satisfaction of looking away. As he got beside the boy's desk, the kid threw a plastic pen at him. It almost hit his face but missed and fell on the floor. Zander stopped and stepped on it. He continued to look at Jair as he put all his weight on the pen. As soon as he heard the case crack, he sat down in the empty desk. A few kids were staring at Jair and laughing.

He knew he'd made an enemy. But in every school he'd ever attended, there was always one kid who wanted to put him down. Nothing ever seemed to make these bullies back off. He'd tried being friendly or ignoring them, but it seemed like they always needed to show off. He didn't feel like getting into it in another school. But after all, the kid had started it.

CHAPTER 3

JAIR

Jair could not believe what had just happened. He'd been so excited to see Keisha after their chat last night. But then she walked in with some new guy. They were laughing, and she seemed so happy. He was dressed in girly colors. No one at Cap Cent ever wore purple pants and a bright blue T-shirt. No one. He'd tried to make a joke about how stupid the guy looked. That's all it was—a joke. He thought Keisha and the other kids would laugh. But Keisha took the new guy's side. She treated Jair like they weren't even friends. And the new guy—what was up with him? So what if he was tall and looked like he worked out. He was dressed like a girl. Wear girl colors, you must be a girl. And making the other kids laugh by breaking his pen? *Not smart, homes. Not smart to take on Jair Nobles.*

Jair felt the rage that always washed over him when anyone dissed him. Through the years, he'd made sure everyone knew how tough he was. Every so often, he'd add to his reputation by actually punching someone. It had been a while since he had to set someone straight.

He had a look that he'd practiced in front of the mirror. He looked right in someone's eyes with his lip curled up in a sneer. There was no one at Cap Cent who didn't look away when he flashed the look. But this new kid was different. He not only didn't look away, he flashed Jair a look of his own. Jair knew throwing the pen was immature, but so what? The guy had to be taught a lesson. He needed to see that Jair was someone to fear. And that Keisha Jackson was off limits.

When the bell rang, the students left the room for lunch. Jair heard someone calling his name. He turned around to see who it was. Janelle Minnerly. He walked faster.

He didn't want to walk with Janelle. Since last year, she had always tried to get with him.

As if he would ever be interested in her. She was everything Keisha was not. Where Keisha was thin and fit, Janelle was big and flabby. Keisha dressed well, and it was obvious her family had some money. Janelle wore clothes that were too tight and looked like they'd been picked up at a thrift shop. And while Keisha's hair and skin were always perfect, Janelle just looked rough.

Jair wasn't the only boy Janelle tried to get with. Actually, she'd be with any guy who showed her any attention. There were Cap Cent guys who laughed about having messed around with her. She lived near the school. Sometimes she would take a guy to her house during the day while her mother was at work. Never the same guy. She was the school joke.

But it was only the coolest guys, like the football players, who could be with her and still look cool. Guys on Jair's level ran the danger of looking like they really liked her. He didn't want to have anything to do with her. He didn't even like to stand beside her. She was so big that she made him look even smaller.

When he heard Janelle's voice again, he knew he was trapped.

"I know you heard me calling you," she said. "I was yelling all the way down the hall!"

"What do you want?" he asked meanly.

"I just wanted to tell you that my mom works weekends, and I'm thinking of having a party on Saturday. Wanna come?"

"You gonna have beer?" Jair asked. He'd never actually been to a party where parents weren't home. It seemed like beer was something she should serve.

"I will if I can find someone to buy it for us," she said. "Do you know anyone?"

"Nah. Why don't you post something online?" he answered.

"Maybe," she said. "Do you wanna eat lunch with me today? Like maybe at my house?"

"Are you serious?" Jair said incredulously. "No way!" He shook his head. "Not gonna happen, Janelle. Now leave me alone." Jair ignored the hurt look on her face. He turned and ran.

CHAPTER 4

ZANDER

The ringing of the lunch bell brought back such bad memories for Zander. Every first day at a new school was the same: happy students eating lunch together, and the new kid eating alone. The students at Cap Central seemed pretty friendly, but until he knew them better, he wasn't going to join them in the cafeteria. He knew that every school had its own divisions, with jocks at one table, smart kids at another, gamers at another—and a large section of kids without friends sitting alone and miserable.

He waited a while to let the crowds filter down. Then he got in line. The lunch looked like every school lunch he'd ever had. The meat and potatoes were an unnatural shade of yellow. Nothing very healthy—until he saw that there was a decent salad bar. He piled some salad on his plate and went off in search of a place to sit.

He saw a door leading to the outside and opened it. There was an enclosed courtyard, complete with picnic tables. The door shut behind him, and he started to head for a table.

Too late, he realized he wasn't alone.

Jair and three other guys had gotten there before him.

CHAPTER 5

JAIR

Jair had asked Luther Ransome, Chance Ruffin, and Thomas Porter to meet him in the court-yard. He grabbed a tray from the cafeteria and went outside. His friends were already seated at the picnic table, eating their lunches.

"So did anybody see Zander Peterson, the new kid who started today?" Jair asked. None of them had. "Well, I don't think he likes girls," he lied. "So watch yourself in the restroom."

"Oh man!" Luther Ransome said. "Just what we need. Another member of the drama club."

"Seriously!" Chance said. "Just once, couldn't someone transfer in here who was a fullback at their old school?"

"Some of the girls were going gaga over him already," Jair lied. "Even Neecy Bethune," he said to Luther, naming a girl he knew the football player had always been interested in.

"He needs to be schooled," Luther said angrily. "I don't care if he's gay or not, he stays away from our girls."

"I know, right?" Jair said innocently. "In fact—"

Right then the door to the courtyard opened and Zander walked out. His head was down, so at first he didn't notice the group of guys sitting on a picnic table.

"Here she is," Jair said loudly. "Here's the new girl I was telling you about."

Zander looked up but didn't say anything for a moment.

"Seriously?" Zander said finally, eating some salad from the tray he had brought outside with him. "Is that the best you can do?"

"You know, I don't know how they felt where you used to live, but we don't like fags here," Jair said.

"I guess no one likes you, then," Zander said.

"What did you say?" Jair asked, hopping down off the table. "Are you calling me a fag?"

"Just sayin'," Zander said, eating his salad. He did not take his eyes off Jair and his friends.

Right then the bell rang, indicating the end of lunch.

"This ain't over," Jair said, walking toward the doors.

"Name the time and place," Zander said softly, but loud enough for Jair to hear.

"You say something, fag?" Jair asked, turning around.

"Leave me alone, bro," Zander said. "I have no beef with you, so just let it go."

"I'm not your bro," Jair said. "But maybe we should get this settled. Meet me on the hill after school. We'll talk it out." The hill was behind the school. Cap Cent kids gathered there to hang out. From the hill, they could look out over D.C.

"Hmm. Let me think about that," Zander said. *I don't need this. It's only the first day of school.* "Okay, I've thought about it. No thanks."

He threw his plate in the trash can by the door and started to walk back inside. Luther, Jair, Thomas, and Chance stood in front of the door, blocking his exit.

"Really?" Zander said, pushing past the

group in order to get into the building. Thomas Porter shoved back and Zander stumbled.

Thomas laughed at him cruelly.

Zander put up his hands in mock surrender and walked inside.

"This ain't over!" Jair shouted to his back.

"So you said," Zander said, turning toward Jair. "Look, I don't know what your problem is, but I don't want to fight you. So let it go."

"You better watch your back," Jair said. The new guy's lack of fear enraged him. No one had ever stood up to him like that before. Without being able to intimidate him, Jair didn't know how to make the guy understand that Jair was the boss.

CHAPTER 6

ZANDER

The next morning, Zander tried to tone down his clothes. He pulled out a black V-neck sweater and some black jeans. His dad was already gone when he left the house to walk to school.

"Hey, Zander. Wait up!" Zander stopped on K Street and waited. Ferg, the guy from Spanish class, and another guy were just turning onto K from Seventeenth Street.

"Hi," he said to the boy he didn't know. "I'm Zander."

"Carlos Garcia," the Hispanic-looking kid said, extending his hand. "Heard you started yesterday. Sucks to be new, doesn't it?"

"Actually, I'm pretty used to it," Zander said. "But, yeah, it does."

"I moved middle of last year when my

grandfather got sick. That first month was so bad. Depending on the day, I felt either invisible or like I was on stage."

"Think I'd rather be invisible," Zander said with a laugh.

"Hey, guys!"

Zander turned and saw Keisha Jackson. She was as hot as he remembered. She was wearing tight blue jeans and a pale yellow sweater.

"Hey, Keisha Jackson," he said. "One of maybe two names I remember from yesterday!"

"You'll know all our names soon," Keisha said. "This school is big, but after a while it doesn't seem that way."

"That's because you learned every name when you ran for president!" Ferg said. "The rest of us are slackers."

"President of what?" Zander asked.

"The student government association," Keisha said with an embarrassed shrug.

"That's pretty impressive," Zander said. "Unfortunately, there's one other name I remember from yesterday. Jair. What's his story?" Zander asked as the four of them stood in front of the school.

"He's a little punk," Carlos said.

"I'd say more of a thug," Ferg added. "Or at least a thug wannabe. Why? What'd he do?"

Zander didn't want to make more of his conversation with Jair than he needed to. "He just seemed to have an instant problem with me."

"Well, watch out for him," Ferg said. "He's stupid but he's tough. And he's a hater of anybody not like him."

"You mean anybody not dumb and ugly," Carlos said with a smirk.

Ferg was clearly embarrassed. "Just … you know. Watch out for him. He's … he beat up a gay kid last year. The kid wouldn't say who did it, but everyone knew it was Jair. I mean, don't worry about him, but—"

"Hey, Ferg!" Eva, the girl from Spanish class, came puffing up behind them. "I've been screaming my head off," she said, rising on her tiptoes to kiss Ferg on the cheek. "What have you been talking about so seriously?"

"Jair Nobles," Ferg said. "He gave Zander a hard time yesterday."

"Not surprising," Eva said, rolling her eyes.

"Remember when he beat Brad up last year? But don't worry. The rest of us are okay. We're very tolerant."

Tolerant? Zander wondered. "Okay, good to hear," he said.

"Oh, speaking of tolerant, I almost forgot!" Keisha said to the group. "We have to brainstorm a school focus project for the year. I'm not coming up with anything, and I need ideas!"

"How about a shorter school year?" Ferg suggested.

"Seriously. I have to present my idea to Mrs. Hess next week, and I have nada. I need help!"

They reached the door of the school. Joss White joined them. Carlos put his arm around her.

"Hi, sweetie!" she said. "Help with what?" she asked Keisha.

"I need ideas for the school focus project," Keisha said. "Seems like all the easy ones were done in the past few years."

"Hmm. I'll think about it. Let's talk at lunch," Joss said. She turned to Zander. "You came back for another day!"

"I did!" he said. "But I tried wearing black so I would fit in."

Eva looked him up and down. "Sorry, still not right," she said. "Still too stylish for D.C."

"So what can I do?" he asked, amused.

"Not much you can do, I'm afraid," Joss said, shaking her head. "You're just too gorgeous for Cap Cent. But we'll let you eat lunch with us anyway," she added. "Meet us in the front hallway by the trophy case. That's where our gang eats. Keisha, we'll help you with your project then. Promise."

Eva and Ferg walked down the hall. Zander realized his first class was in the same direction—this even/odd schedule was throwing him off—so he followed them. He was embarrassed at the flattery. Gorgeous? Not hardly!

" 'Too gorgeous?' " Ferg was saying to Eva. "I can't believe Joss said that to him. What's up with you girls?"

Eva looked surprised. "He *is* gorgeous! But I heard he doesn't like girls, so it's not like he's gonna hit on us or anything!"

Zander was stunned. The whole school

thought he didn't like girls? He had no idea how that rumor got started. Or how to correct it. So much for finding a girlfriend. He shook his head in disgust. In two short days, he'd angered the school bully and been mislabeled as gay. Must be some sort of record.

Zander went to the trophy case at lunch. Cap Cent was so large that not all of the students could eat in the cafeteria. Instead, they were allowed to eat pretty much anywhere they wanted, as long as they stayed on school grounds.

He found Ferg, Carlos, and Joss among a group of about eight to ten other students. Ferg made the introductions. After several names, Zander couldn't keep them straight. Keisha Jackson sat on one side of him and Eva on the other. Eva began quizzing him good-naturedly. She asked about where he lived, what music he listened to, what kinds of movies he liked.

"Eva, leave the guy alone!" one of the boys finally said. "Sorry on behalf of the rest of Cap Cent," he said, extending his hand. "Durand Butler, in case you're overloaded on names."

Zander laughed as they shook hands. "No worries," he said.

"Is your name short for Alexander?" Keisha asked.

"No, just Zander," he answered. "A little quirk on my dad's part. He's Alexander but didn't want to look conceited by naming me after himself."

"What does your mom think about it?" Keisha asked.

Zander got serious. "I don't know. I've never asked her. I'll have to run that by her when she gets back. She's been in Afghanistan for a year, and she doesn't get to call home much."

Everyone was quiet. "Sorry," Durand said. "That must be tough."

"Yeah, well, it is what it is," Zander said.

The rest of lunch was filled with chatter. Then the bell rang and everyone stood up.

"Wait—we didn't talk about the focus project!" Keisha said. "I have to come up with some ideas by next week."

"We'll talk later," Eva said, picking up her books.

"See you all later," Joss said, walking off.

"So much for all the help they promised," Keisha said, shaking her head. "I don't know what I'm going to do. I really, really need some ideas."

"I could help you, but I don't know the kinds of projects this school does," Zander said. "But we could talk about it sometime if you'd like," he added.

"That would be great." She smiled up at him. Zander's heart skipped a beat. "But we'd better not be late for class," Keisha said. "Where do you go next?"

Zander pulled out his schedule. "Biology in three forty-six," he said. "I'm guessing that's two floors up."

"Yeah, it is. I can walk with you," Keisha said. "I'm going that way." They started walking down the hall.

"Keisha!" a voice called out.

They stopped and Zander turned around. Jair and four other guys were behind them.

"What do you want, Jair?" Keisha said.

"I need to talk to you, girl," Jair said.

"Not now," Keisha said. "I'm showing Zander to class."

"I can talk to you, Jair," a girl said. She was standing near the lockers, outside of Jair's group of friends. Zander had never seen her before. She was a big girl—much taller than Jair and about fifty pounds heavier.

Zander and Keisha started walking down the hall. "Get lost," he heard Jair say to the girl. Then he yelled, "Forget it, Keisha. He doesn't like girls."

"Oh, Zander, I'm so sorry you had to hear that," Keisha said. "He's not the most tolerant person in the world."

Zander stopped. "Look, I need to set the record straight here. I'm not—"

"Hey, Brad! Someone I want you to meet," Keisha said. "Brad, meet Zander Peterson. Zander, this is Brad."

"How you doing?" Zander said, shaking Brad's hand.

"Great, man," Brad answered. They stopped outside room 346. "You in this class?"

"I am," Zander said. "How is it?"

"Not bad for a science class. Doctor Miller is pretty interesting." They walked into the class. Zander stopped by the teacher's desk to introduce himself.

When class was over, Brad was waiting in the hallway. "Hey, don't know if you're interested, but there's a group of us who get together once a week on Thursdays to talk about diversity issues here at Cap Cent," he said. "We meet in the cafeteria."

"Thanks," Zander said noncommittally. "I'll think about it."

Brad stopped suddenly. "You're not actually gay, are you?"

"Sorry, no," Zander said.

"Wow, how did that rumor get started?" Brad asked.

"Truth? I think it's because I wore an aqua T-shirt yesterday," Zander said with a laugh. "Some punk named Jair called me a girl. That's apparently all it took!"

"Watch out for him," Brad said seriously. "He's a hater. He sucker-punched me last year for no reason. Waited for me after school and jumped me."

"What's his problem?" Zander asked.

"Who knows? Maybe it's because he's short," Brad said. "Actually, the rumor back in middle school was that his father knocks him around.

So maybe that's how he's used to working stuff out. In any case, somebody to avoid."

"I can take him," Zander said. "But thanks for the warning."

"Here's another one," Brad said. "If you want folks to realize you're not gay, you're going to have to dress down a bit. You look too ... magazine-y."

"Sheesh. This is what happens when you move from the West Coast," Zander said. "But thanks."

He looked at the room number by where they'd ended up. "Oh, this is me," he said. "Computer applications."

"See you around!" Brad said.

Zander introduced himself to the teacher and took a seat in the back. He was pretty lost throughout the class since he hadn't had much computer science at his previous schools. He had always gotten good grades, but this class would be a challenge.

The teacher noticed. "Zander, stay after class a bit so I can figure out where the best placement would be for you," he said.

After class, Zander talked to the teacher

for a while. By the time he left, the halls were nearly empty. He walked out the side door of the school onto Bladensburg Road and started for home. When he got past the school parking lot, he saw a crowd of kids standing on the sidewalk where Bladensburg met Maryland Avenue. He continued walking toward them. He wondered what was going on. They were blocking his path. He started to step into the street to go around them when he heard someone call his name. Jair walked out from the middle of the group. He was smiling a sly smile. He stood in the center of the sidewalk with his arms folded across his chest.

Zander looked behind him, hoping to see a teacher or security guard. But there was no one of authority. When he turned around, he saw that the crowd had begun to surround him and Jair. Even if someone at the school had looked over in his direction, the crowd of students would have blocked the view. Several students had taken out cell phones and were starting to film, Zander suspected. With a sinking feeling, Zander knew he was going to be jumped. He tried to step around the group, but his path was blocked.

Jair began walking slowly toward him, a nasty grin on his face. "You need to understand a few facts about our school," he said. "First, we don't like fags. Second, we don't like fags who get too friendly with our girls."

"No problem," Zander said, trying to keep his tone light. "I'll stay away from your girlfriends, and you stay away from me."

"Well, see, that's not good enough," Jair said. "Promises, promises. I don't like fags, especially ones that seem to think they're all that. I think you need to be schooled."

"No need," Zander said. "Like I said, I get it. So why don't you let me pass. I'll leave you alone, and you can leave me alone."

Zander's muscles were clenched. His feet moved into a familiar stance: shoulder width apart, left foot slightly forward, weight on the balls of his feet.

"Nah, I've been thinking about it," Jair said. "You *need* to be schooled. And we want to make sure all of Cap Cent knows what a girl you are."

Zander dropped his backpack and held his hands up in surrender. "Look, I don't want to fight you, man," he said. "Let's just let it go.

You're clearly the man around here, and I'm just the new guy. I won't mess with you or your girls." Slowly, he tucked his chin down toward his chest. He bounced slightly on the balls of his feet, making sure not to lock his knees.

"That's right," Jair said. "But I want a record of why you'll think about it next time you try talking to one of our girls." He planted his feet, stuck out his chest, and raised his chin aggressively. Zander almost laughed. Jair was a good six inches shorter than he was. And the way he was standing showed he didn't know how to fight.

"I don't want to fight you," Zander said. "Please don't do this."

"'Please don't do this,'" Jair mocked in a high voice. "Please! Oh, pretty please!" He turned to some of the guys standing behind him. "I told you he sounded like a girl!"

Suddenly, his right arm shot out toward Zander's face. Zander had seen it coming and twisted his body so the shot went harmlessly past his shoulder.

"Look, I'm warning you," Zander said, his voice cold. "Don't do this. You don't know who you're messing with. I don't want to fight you.

I want you to stop. I'll walk away if you'll just move so I can get past."

"I don't know who I'm messing with?" Jair smirked. "You look like a girl, and I'll bet you fight like a girl."

He jabbed again, but Zander deflected it. Then Jair tried again, using his left hand. Zander dodged the hit. He could see that Jair was getting frustrated. Zander desperately hoped for a cop to drive by or a security guard to show up on the scene.

"Okay, now let's just let it go," he said, holding up his hands. "You made your point."

"Yeah, here's my point!" Jair said, charging toward him. Fists flailing, he pounded on Zander. A couple of Jair's blows actually connected but didn't do much harm.

Zander raised his left hand to protect his face. Jair let loose with a huge right hook. Although it missed his face, it connected with Zander's shoulder. It was as if that punch flipped a switch. Zander led with his right but jabbed with his left. He aimed for Jair's shoulders and ribs in order to minimize the damage.

He twisted his leg around Jair's leg and

brought him down. As he threw his body over Jair's, he was dimly aware of Jair yelling, "Okay! Okay!"

Zander's anger had taken over, and he continued punching. All those years of MMA training in gyms around the country took over, and it was as if his body had a life of its own. Finally, he noticed that Jair wasn't moving.

Zander slowly got up and tried to catch his breath.

"I asked you not to fight me, you little punk," he said coldly, looking down on Jair. "I told you to walk away. You had this coming. Now leave me alone. Next time, I'll hurt you bad. Hear me?"

Jair didn't look up. He nodded silently.

"I want to hear it," Zander yelled. "Say it for the cameras."

"I hear ya," Jair said.

"Anybody else want a piece of me?" Zander asked, looking at the others. None of them would make eye contact. They all shook their heads. He suspected that some of the students were still filming.

"Good. Now leave me alone and let me pass," Zander demanded. Some of the guys moved out of the way, and he was able to get into the street.

"That dude can fight!" someone said behind him.

"He kicked Jair's butt!" someone else added. Zander knew he had made an enemy for life. He also knew it was just a matter of time before he got suspended.

JAIR

Jair wanted to cry. Not so much from the pummeling, though that hurt like heck. But more from the humiliation. He had thought he could threaten Zander and maybe make him look weak. He wanted Keisha and the rest of the school to hear about the fight and know he had put the new kid down. He hadn't been prepared for someone who actually knew how to fight. That guy totally made a fool of him. The people surrounding him weren't exactly his friends. He knew they would turn on him in a minute if they thought he was weak.

Slowly, he got up and dusted off his jeans. "I guess you got told," Chance Ruffin said with a smirk.

"Seriously, homes," Thomas Porter said. "I thought you were gonna school him."

"It ain't over," Jair said, trying to sound tough. "Anybody can sucker punch. I'll show him he doesn't mess with me."

"Whatever," Thomas answered with a laugh. "Thanks for the text telling us to show up here. Text me again the next time you plan to get your butt kicked."

"So I guess he's not gay," Luther Ransome said. "I've never known a gay guy who could fight like that!"

"Nah, he's gay all right," Jair lied. "Anyway, that wasn't fighting. He didn't even hit me. I just tripped."

"Really?" Luther said with sarcasm. "Guess I'll watch the video later to see how well you faked getting hit. 'Cause it sure looked real to me."

The group slowly walked off. Jair thought he was alone. Then he saw a girl standing nearby. It was Janelle.

"Do you want to come over so I can give you some ice for your face?" she asked. "That will keep you from getting a bruise."

"How do you know?" Jair asked, rubbing his jaw.

" 'Cause it's what I do," she said. She didn't explain further, but she didn't have to. Jair knew she probably got hit at home, just like he did.

"C'mon. I've got something to show you," Janelle said. "I just live over there."

"Janelle, for the last time, leave me alone!" he said angrily. "Can't you just take a hint?"

"I can get you a gun."

For a moment, Jair felt like the earth had stopped spinning. He didn't even breathe.

"What did you say?" he asked.

"A gun," she repeated. "Now do you want to come to my house or not?"

Jair didn't know what to think. Right now, he couldn't think straight.

"Yeah. No. I don't know. Maybe some other day. Not today. I just wanna go home."

"Whatever," Janelle said. "Just remember what I said about the gun."

Jair started walking toward his apartment. His head was pounding. The beating he had taken from Zander was part of it. But mostly he could hear Janelle's words in his mind.

A gun. A gun. A gun.

He needed to think. He wished he could go somewhere besides his apartment. He knew he looked bad. There was blood on his shirt. It would be bad enough trying to avoid his little brothers' questions. If his father was home, he'd be in big trouble. There was no way his father wouldn't recognize the signs that Jair had been in a fight.

He hopped a Metrobus going north on Bladensburg. He took it a few stops and walked to his apartment on Raum Street. He opened the apartment door. Royce and Marcel were on the couch, their eyes glued to the TV. A cartoon was playing with the volume turned up loud.

"I'm telling Mom," Royce said without taking his eyes off the screen. "You're supposed to be here to take care of us when we get home from school."

"You tell Mom and I'll pound your butt," Jair said. "I had stuff to do after school."

"Stuff with your girlfriend," Marcel said in a sing-song voice. For a moment Jair thought he meant Janelle. Then he remembered the younger boys teasing him the day before, when they had seen his chat with Keisha. That seemed so long ago. And so unimportant now.

"Just keep it to yourselves," he warned again. "Or you'll be sorry." He went to the bathroom and looked in the mirror. Bruises were already starting to show on his chest and shoulders. Nothing on his face, but his whole upper body looked bad. His ego hurt worse than his bruises. He hated this new kid. He wanted him to die.

Whenever he thought about getting even, his thoughts returned to Janelle's offer. *A gun.* Even just flashing the gun would make Zander understand who he'd messed with.

That night, Jair booted up the family computer. Usually he started getting instant messages as soon as he went online. But tonight? Nothing.

He looked at the list of people who were online at the same time. Luther Ransome, Keisha Jackson, Chance Ruffin, Neecy Bethune, Ferg Ferguson. Even Janelle Minnerly. He sent an instant message to Keisha, but she didn't reply. He tried Luther and Chance. Still nothing.

He tried playing a few games online, but his heart wasn't in it. He was about to sign off when he got a message from Janelle.

"Sorry 2 tell u this, but there's a video of u in the fight. U should c it. I hope he didn't hurt u. He cheated. Think about what I said."

She included a link to a YouTube video. With a sick feeling in his stomach, Jair clicked on it. He watched the video in horror. It was the fight, but it was edited to make it look even worse than it had been. Whoever had made the video did things like show Jair protecting his head and saying "okay, okay, okay" over and over. Zander's punches were sped up and repeated, so it looked like they went on forever. The whole thing was set to music; a song whose chorus was something like "fight like a girl."

Jair went to his room and crawled into his bed. He had no idea who made and posted the video. But only his so-called friends had been at the fight. If Jair's friends would do something like that, what would people who weren't his friends do?

He couldn't go back to school to face all his classmates. He needed to teach Zander Peterson a lesson. He had to show the world that he was strong and tough. Not like the loser in the video.

Jair knew Zander would pummel him in a fistfight. And he would be humiliated all over again. But even a trained fighter couldn't win against a gun.

CHAPTER 8

ZANDER

When Zander arrived at school the next morning, he noticed a difference. Instead of being the strange new kid, it seemed like he was being stared at with respect. Small groups of students were talking closely, sometimes pointing at him as he passed.

He saw Carlos and Ferg, who waved him over. "You okay?" Ferg asked. "Hear you went a few rounds with Jair yesterday."

"News does travel fast in this place," Zander said. "How'd you hear?"

"Lots of traffic last night," Carlos said. "You probably don't have anybody's Facebook or Twitter handles yet, so you most likely didn't see the video."

"What video?" Zander asked.

"Somebody filmed the fight and posted it on YouTube. It's a classic," Carlos said with a smile.

"Yeah, I missed that for sure," Zander sighed. He didn't want to tell them that his father forbade him from using any social media. No Facebook, no Twitter, no YouTube. He had no way of seeing what everybody else at Cap Cent had apparently already seen. "How'd I look?"

"You kicked his butt!" Keisha Jackson said, joining the group. "But how are you doing? Did he hurt you?"

She put her hand on Zander's face and looked closely at him. Her beautiful eyes were filled with concern. He couldn't take his eyes off her.

"I'm okay," he said finally. His voice came out in a funny squeak.

"You don't sound okay!" she said playfully. "Do you need some first aid?"

Yes, he thought. *Touch me again.* "Nah, I'm okay," he said. "A little sore but I'll live."

"Where'd you learn to fight?" Ferg asked.

"Everywhere," Zander said. "My dad thinks it keeps me out of trouble. Wait till he hears about this!"

"I probably shouldn't say this, but I'm glad you kicked Jair's butt," Carlos confessed. "He's a bully. No one ever stands up to him. They're afraid they'll be next on his list. I'm guessing a lot of people are happy about what you did."

"Tell that to my dad when he has to come get me after I get suspended," Zander said, shaking his head. "He's gonna kill me."

Just then, the bell rang. Zander started to walk with Keisha and Ferg to Mr. Guevara's class. She was walking close beside him. It took a minute or two before he realized he was grinning.

Class had only been in session for about fifteen minutes when Mrs. Dominguez, the principal's secretary, called on the classroom phone to ask that Zander come to the office. Zander picked up his books and put them in his backpack. Someone in the class started clapping, and soon the whole class was applauding.

"Class, get control," Mr. Guevara said. *"¡Deténgase! ¡A trabajar!"*

Zander walked slowly to the office. Mrs. Dominguez told him to take a seat. The front door opened and his father walked in, in full uniform. The look on his face made Zander want to run and hide. His father took off his cap and sat down without saying anything. Zander wanted to explain, but he knew it was useless.

Soon, Mrs. Dominguez told them to go into the principal's office. "Colonel Peterson, Zander, welcome. I'm Mrs. Hess," the principal said, standing up at her desk. "And this is Mr. Gable, the school's security guard." She waved a hand toward a large man wearing a uniform. "Please, have a seat."

Zander sat as far from his father as he could. He slouched down in his chair. "Sit up straight!" his father ordered.

Zander immediately sat up. "Yes, sir," he answered.

"Zander, would you like to tell your father why you're here?" Mrs. Hess asked.

"I guess it's because I got in a fight yesterday," Zander said.

He heard his father swear softly.

"Look, I did everything I could to keep from fighting," Zander said desperately. "I don't know what you heard, but I tried walking away. They wouldn't let me pass. That kid, Jair, had it in for me from the moment he saw me. And yesterday, when he started swinging, he wouldn't stop. That's when I pounded him."

"Well, the fight is actually only part of the problem," Mrs. Hess said. "The other part—the part that is even more of a concern—is a video of the fight posted on YouTube. We have zero tolerance toward cyberbullying, and the video crosses the line. The whole thing—the video and the music ..." Mrs. Hess shook her head. "It is offensive and hateful, no matter what Jair did."

Zander was speechless. Did the principal think *he* posted the video?

"Video?" his father asked. "Did you post a video of some kind?"

"No!" Zander said. "How could I have?" He turned back to Mrs. Hess. "Ma'am, I don't know what you're talking about."

"Zander, it will be better for you if you don't lie," Mrs. Hess said. "But since your father obviously hasn't seen the video, let's look at it, shall we?"

She punched some buttons on her computer. Lights shone on a whiteboard, and soon a YouTube video appeared. A song started playing, with a chorus of "I know I'm a girl! I look like a girl! I fight like a girl!" On the screen, Zander was punching Jair over and over again, as Jair covered up his head. The video made it look like Zander was a madman. Like he started the fight and wouldn't let Jair escape.

When the video was over, Mrs. Hess turned to Zander's father. "Colonel Peterson, since Zander obviously hasn't shown you this, you probably don't know that it's already been viewed several thousand times. Students have texted about it, and there's even a new Facebook page called 'Jair Nobles fights like a girl.' Right before this meeting, there were fifty-six posted comments, with one hundred twenty-three 'likes.' "

"Son, do you know what she's talking about?" Colonel Peterson asked Zander.

"Honestly? No," Zander answered. "Mrs. Hess, I couldn't post a video to YouTube if my life depended on it—if that's what I'm being accused of. I'm not allowed to use any social media. I don't even have a smartphone. I didn't do this, I wouldn't know how to do this, and this isn't the way the fight happened. Whoever posted it edited it to make it look much worse than it was."

"We actually know that the last part of what you said is the truth," Mr. Gable spoke up. "There's a security camera on top of the school. We viewed the footage from yesterday. There's no sound, but we could see that you were trying to get away. Until he started punching and you punched back."

"Could we see that tape please?" Colonel Peterson asked. "The tape that shows what really happened."

Zander looked at him in surprise. He almost sounded like he wasn't angry. "No, son, you're still in trouble," his father said, as if reading his mind. "But I'd like to see how the whole thing started."

Mrs. Hess punched some more buttons. A grainy video popped up on the whiteboard. The camera was behind the crowd. It was high enough to capture the action in the center. Although the figures were small, you could clearly see what was happening.

The video played silently. For the first forty seconds, Zander stood with his hands up, trying several times to walk past Jair and his friends. It was clear they would not let him leave. As he walked toward them, they moved closer together, blocking his way. Suddenly, Jair threw a punch. Zander turned and deflected it. This happened several times. Then Zander again raised his hands. Jair punched, and Zander's head snapped back. His hands came down, and he began punching back until Jair covered his head. As soon as Jair wasn't a threat, Zander quit punching. The boys spoke briefly. Then Zander left.

Mrs. Hess switched off the computer. "Who filmed the fight?" she asked.

"How would I know that?" Zander asked angrily. "Look, I just got here two days ago. I know maybe two or three kids' names. Jair came after me from day one, making all sorts of bigoted comments. If you have so much zero tolerance, why is he allowed to get away with that kind of hate talk?"

"What kind of hate talk?" Mrs. Hess asked. "How did he come after you?"

"Ask him," Zander said bitterly. "He seems to think I'm something I'm not."

"Son, if you have something to say, I think you'd better just say it," Colonel Peterson said sternly.

"Forget it," Zander said. "Do what you have

to do to me about the fight. But I didn't make that video. I don't know the names of the kids who filmed it. I didn't ask for this to happen, but he wouldn't let it go."

"That's actually obvious," Mrs. Hess said. "Nevertheless, as I told you, we do not allow students to be bullied over the Internet. The YouTube tape clearly was an attempt to humiliate Jair."

"There were dozens of kids there! And he—" Zander protested.

"Ma'am, if I could speak?" Colonel Peterson said.

Mrs. Hess nodded.

"I'm not one to excuse my boy for any wrong behavior. None of us could hear what was being said in that security tape, but it seemed clear to me that Zander was trying to do the right thing. Those boys wouldn't let him pass. What would you have had him do?"

Mrs. Hess was quiet for a moment. "You should have reasoned with Jair ... talked to him about the problem." The principal sighed. "Though that's not very realistic, is it?" she said thoughtfully. "I get your point, Colonel Peterson.

Today is Wednesday. How about if Zander goes home now and doesn't come in for the rest of the week? You come back in on Monday, and that will be all."

Colonel Peterson was shaking his head. "But it will show up as a suspension, right?" he asked. "This isn't right, ma'am. He shouldn't have that on his record just because it's the easiest way for the school to handle it. He was the victim here. Don't make him more of a victim."

Mrs. Hess played with a pencil. "Okay. I believe that you had nothing to do with the video. And I think you *were* ambushed," she said. "But I need to make sure this problem between you and Jair doesn't go any further. If I don't suspend you," she continued, "you are not to discuss the fight, the video, or this meeting with anyone. The incident, as far as you are concerned, is closed. Is that understood?"

Zander couldn't believe it. No punishment. That had to be a first. "I understand," he said.

"I also have to insist that you have no contact with Jair whatsoever. No conversation in the hall, no threats of retaliation, no nothing. Is that clear?" Mrs. Hess continued.

Zander nodded.

"Ma'am? If I can ask, what will happen to the other boy involved?" Colonel Peterson asked.

"Jair will be suspended," Mrs. Hess said. "As for the YouTube video, we'll have to investigate further to find out who is responsible. It's obviously been edited to humiliate Jair. I told you we have a zero tolerance policy toward cyberbullying. We will take appropriate action once our investigation is concluded."

Colonel Peterson stood up and shook hands with Mrs. Hess. "I appreciate you being accommodating toward my boy," he said. "You didn't have to be so flexible, and I want you to know we're grateful."

"Your son seems to have a good head on his shoulders, Colonel Peterson," Mrs. Hess said. "Zander, I hope to see a lot more of you, but under happier circumstances. Welcome to Capital Central, by the way. I think you'll be a real asset to our school."

"Ma'am," Colonel Peterson said, nodding his head. He and Zander walked out of the office.

"Thanks, Dad," Zander said when they were in the outer office. "I appreciate it."

"Son, when you do wrong, you deserve to be punished," Colonel Peterson said. "In this case, you didn't do anything wrong. It would have been unfair to punish you. I'll see you tonight."

Zander watched him leave. Then he turned to go back to class, nearly bumping into Mr. Gable.

"Zander, I've got some advice for you, son," Mr. Gable said gruffly.

Zander stood and waited for the lecture he figured was coming.

"You're rolling back too far on your left foot. Your hips were way out of line. That's why some of your punches went off like that. If you distribute your weight more evenly, you'll have better balance. What are you? Middleweight?"

Zander was speechless. A fight lesson was the last thing he expected.

"Welterweight actually," he said.

"There's a group of kids who get together after school in the weight room here," Mr. Gable said. "They lift weights and use the speed and punching bags. A couple of them do a little sparring. If you're interested, you're welcome to join us. I don't know if you're fighting now, but it's a good way to stay in shape until you find yourself a gym to join."

"Thanks, sir. I'll check it out," Zander said. Mr. Gable held up his fist. Zander fist-bumped him before they both walked off.

Zander walked back to class, shaking his head. Capital Central High School was proving to be more interesting than he could have ever imagined.

CHAPTER 9

JAIR

By the time his alarm rang the next morning, Jair had already been awake for an hour. He had hardly slept. His whole body hurt, and he couldn't get comfortable. He couldn't quit thinking about the video and how weak it made him look. There was no way he was going to school.

There were a lot of guys there who'd be happy he got taken down. Weak guys. The ones he'd schooled over the past few years. And the ones who thought they might be next in line. He knew they were going to make his life miserable until he set them straight about how tough he was.

He went into the bathroom and made loud gagging noises. Then he got back in bed. His mother soon came in. She had a worried look on her face.

"Are you sick?" she asked.

"I guess," he answered. "I just threw up," he lied.

"Well, you'd better stay home, then," she said. "You don't look good," she added. "I can see you're not feeling like yourself."

No kidding. I got the crap beat out of me, Jair thought. He turned to face the wall. "I think I'll just go back to sleep," he said, closing his eyes.

His mother kissed him on the forehead. "You call me if you need anything," she said.

Jair dozed while he heard his brothers getting ready for school. Soon the apartment was quiet. He got out of bed and got dressed. He checked his cell phone and sent a text message to Janelle.

"I want it. Can u meet me at ur house at 11?"

While he waited for her response, he sat at the kitchen table and ate some cereal. His phone buzzed with a message from Janelle.

"Sure. I'll tell my brother cuz it's his. C u at 11."

He pushed his phone away. Suddenly, he heard the sound of someone coming up the stairs leading to his apartment. He raced into his room and tore off his shirt and pants, scrambling to put back on the T-shirt and basketball shorts he slept in. He jumped into bed and turned toward the wall, pretending to be asleep.

"Don't know if there's any food in here, but at least I've got a bottle," his father's voice said as the front door opened.

Jair could not hear the response. He counted at least three other voices, one of which was a woman's. He didn't know why they were at his apartment, but he figured he'd better let his father know the place wasn't empty.

"Dad? Dad?" he called out.

"What the—" his father said. He threw open the door to Jair's room. "What? Why are you here?" he asked angrily.

"I'm sick," Jair said. "Mom said I should stay home from school."

"Well, I've got some people out here, and we have to talk. About some business," he added. "So you have to stay in here till I leave. But since you're so 'sick,'" his father dragged the word out with a sneer, "that shouldn't be a problem."

Jair's father walked out and shut the door behind him. Jair looked at the clock on his dresser. Ten thirty. He wondered how long his father would be there. If he was to meet Janelle at her house at eleven, he had to leave soon.

Fifteen minutes later he was panicking. He needed to text Janelle. He couldn't get away. He looked for his phone. Where was it? With horror, he realized he didn't have it. He remembered leaving it on the kitchen table when he was eating his cereal.

His father and his friends kept talking and laughing. Jair could hear the sound of ice cubes in glasses. It sounded like they were having a party. He got up and looked out the window. There was an alley that ran behind his house. He knew it was too far down to jump, but he considered it anyway. Sometimes there were garbage cans back there, but today there weren't any under his window. Without something to land on, he'd almost certainly get hurt. He knew being late would make a lousy impression on Janelle's brother. But he was trapped in his room and couldn't leave.

At 11:10, he heard his cell phone ringing. His father let it ring until it stopped. It immediately started ringing again. This time, Jair heard his father say, "I'll just turn it off."

He lay down on his bed and pulled the covers up. Now he really did feel sick. Janelle and her brother would think he was ignoring them. He might never have another chance to buy a gun. And without a gun, he had no way to re-establish himself as a tough guy.

By noon, Jair could tell his father was drunk. His voice was too loud, his words were slurred, and he was arguing with at least one of his guests. Jair was actually glad his father had friends over. Had it been just the two of them, he knew his father would have started picking a fight. Lying in bed, Jair got sleepy. He put a pillow over his head to block the noise and fell asleep.

He woke up when his father burst through the bedroom door. He was holding a cell phone to his ear. "Tell me that again?" he said. "My kid did what?"

The school. The fight. Jair hadn't given it a thought. He was in trouble for sure.

His father never took his eyes off him as he listened to the person on the other end. "Uh huh," he said. "Seriously? ... No, that's right," and finally, "I understand."

He hung up the phone and slowly put it in his pocket.

"Any guesses as to what that was about?" he asked coldly.

"Probably the school calling to say I was in a fight," Jair answered. He hated how scared his voice was. There was no one he was scared of more than his father. "But it wasn't my fault! I mean, this new kid, he—"

His father put up his hand to stop him. "Be careful, son. Apparently the whole thing is on YouTube. So I can verify every word out of your mouth."

Jair was silent. "Guy set me up," he said finally. "Acting like some sort of sissy. Talking to my friends ... to girls. Flirted. Turns out he's a trained fighter."

"So he schooled your ass?" his father said with a smirk. "Hope my friends don't see that video. Find out what kind of a girl my kid turned out to be."

Jair was crushed. Even his father thought he was weak. Well, he'd be one of the most surprised when Jair got the gun and made things right.

"Meanwhile, you gotta pay the consequences. School suspended you for three days, but that's just them. Me? I think you gotta learn a lesson. Turn around."

His father began unbuckling his belt. The one with the huge buckle. Jair wanted to protest, but he knew it wouldn't help. He turned around. As the belt whooshed down, he steeled himself not to cry. He'd learned the hard way that crying just made his father hit him harder.

After Zander Peterson, his father was next on his list.

CHAPTER 10

ZANDER

Zander stopped by the weight room after school. The place was busy. There were guys using the speed bags and punching bags, a few were jumping rope, and several were lifting weights.

"Hey, Zander, come on in," Mr. Gable said. "Guys, this is Zander Peterson. He's got a wicked right hook."

The other boys said hello.

"You do any lifting?" Mr. Gable asked.

"Some," Zander answered. "Looks like you've got some nice equipment. None of my other schools had a weight room I could use. It was restricted to athletics."

"We're pretty lucky," Mr. Gable agreed. "Anyway, look around and use anything you'd like. I'm here every Tuesday, Wednesday, and

Thursday. You can come as often as you like. Your friends too. We're always trying to get the kids who aren't on school teams to use this equipment."

"Thanks," Zander said. He walked over to the speed bag and gave it a tap. It bounced back. He put down his backpack and punched it a bit. Without gloves, he didn't want to hurt his hands. But it felt good to use the bag. It had been a while since he'd worked out.

He picked up his backpack and thanked Mr. Gable. He left the school and was relieved to see that no one was waiting to jump him.

That evening, Zander had a video chat with his mother. He told her about the fight and how the school had not punished him.

"I'm happy at how it all worked out," she said. "But I'm sorry it had to happen at all. What was his problem?" she asked.

"I'm not sure," Zander said. "First he accused me of being gay. Then he accused me of stealing his girl."

"He sounds a little confused," his mother said, concerned. "But watch out for him. There's nothing more dangerous than a bully who is embarrassed. He's going to think he has something to prove now."

"I know," Zander said. "I just don't understand why every school seems to have one guy who wants to prove he's the toughest."

"There's usually a reason," she said. "He's beat up at home, or he feels insecure for some reason. You look good, you're smart, and kids like you. That can be threatening to someone without your confidence."

"I guess," Zander said.

"So did you steal his girl?" she asked.

"Mom! I just started school a few days ago," Zander replied.

"I'm just kidding, honey," she said. "I just wondered what made him think that. Or that you were gay."

"He thought I was gay because I wore an aqua T-shirt," Zander said. "So I wore black, but apparently I still looked too L.A. He thought I stole his girl because some girl showed me where my class was. But mostly he just wanted to fight me."

"Okay, okay," his mother said. "Calm down. You'll figure it all out. You always do."

They talked some more, and then she said she had to sign off. "But, Zander?" she said.

"Yeah?"

"What's this girl's name?"

"Mom!" he yelled.

His mother laughed hard. "Just yanking your chain, baby," she said. "Wish I could be there to give you some motherly advice. But here's all I got: keep calm and carry on."

"I miss you, Mom," Zander sighed.

"Me too, baby. Be good, okay?"

"I will. You be careful, okay?" Zander said.

"You know it. I'll be home before too long, I promise. Good-night. And sweet dreams."

Zander signed off. He always had mixed emotions after talking to his mother. He was glad to hear from her, but the calls made him miss her even more.

He went into the living room to talk to his father.

"I'm thinking of working out in the school's weight room after school," he said. "Mr. Gable— the security guard you met today—runs the place. I feel like I'm really out of shape."

"Sounds like you kicked that boy to the curb yesterday," his father said.

"Granny Peterson could have whipped that guy," Zander said, shaking his head. "I don't know why people start fights who don't know how to fight."

"Any idea what set him off?" his father asked.

"None. He started in on me the moment I walked into my second class. I think it might be because I walked in with this girl who showed me where the class was."

"You said something in the principal's office about his making bigoted comments. Was this because you're black?"

"Nah, I don't think so," Zander said. "Most everyone in the school is black or Hispanic. I'm not sure what his background is, but I know he's not white."

"So his comments—" his father started to say.

"He called me a ... he called me a slang word for gay," Zander said. "Far as I can tell, it's because I dress differently than the kids here."

"Disappointing that people still use that ugly word," his father said. "Sometimes people act hateful because they're feeling threatened or inferior. Something about you must have set him off. Maybe because you're tall or good looking or something. You were lucky the school saw this thing your way," he continued. "Makes me wonder if the guy has a history of this behavior. But I want to make sure you know to keep well away from him. I don't want him to retaliate."

"Don't worry. I don't want to have anything to do with him," Zander said. "I just hope he leaves me alone."

"Well, watch your back," his father said, picking up the paper. "Looks like you humiliated him in that fight. If he was already feeling inferior, this will just add to his anger. But be kind if you run into him. Whatever makes him act like that, he can't be a very happy guy."

"I'll be careful," Zander assured him. "Thanks, Dad. I'd better go get my homework done."

CHAPTER 11

JAIR

Jair hated being on suspension. He hated school, but it was worse to be home with nothing to do. He watched some TV and played video games, but it wasn't fun. He was so frustrated. He left the apartment for a while and walked around his neighborhood. He didn't know how he could take three days of this boredom.

He needed to call Janelle to apologize for not coming over. But his father had taken away his cell phone as punishment for the fight. Jair searched all over the apartment for it, but he couldn't find it anywhere. He wanted to go to her house, but he knew she'd be at school until about the time when he had to be home to watch his brothers.

His mother left him a list of chores to do

while she was gone. Laundry, dusting, starting dinner. Nothing that he felt like doing. For a while, he lay on his bed thinking about getting revenge against Zander. He held his hand like a gun and aimed at a stain on the ceiling. "Bang," he said. "Bang, bang. You're dead, pretty boy."

He thought about how Keisha would cry. How he'd be there to make her feel better. He figured she'd feel bad at first that Zander had died, but then she would see that Jair was the tougher guy. It was just a matter of time till she was his girlfriend.

"Bang," he said again. "Bang, bang, bang."

He wondered what kind of gun Janelle would get him. He hoped it was a Glock. He stuck one of his mother's wooden spoons in the back of his pants and practiced pulling it out as if it were a gun. He thought about writing a rap song about the shooting but couldn't get beyond, "I gotta gun, now you'd better run."

Finally, his brothers came home. He got them a snack and turned on the TV. His mother came home around six and was pleased to see that he'd started dinner.

After dinner, he helped her clean up. He

said, "You know, I wondered today what I would do if there were a fire or something. Without my phone, I'm sort of stranded."

"Your father said you couldn't have it," his mother lectured.

"Yeah, but this could have been dangerous," Jair whined. "What if something happened with the boys?" He hoped his mother couldn't tell how he was playing her.

"But I don't want to go against your father," she said. Jair hated how scared she looked when she said it. He knew she was as scared of his father as he was. He'd never actually seen his father hit her. But he'd seen his father drag her into their bedroom, slam the door, and scream at her. A few times she had worn sunglasses for a few days.

"Think about it, okay, Mom?" he said. "I was worried when I was watching the boys. I just don't know what I'd do if there was an emergency when I am home with them without a phone."

He turned quickly so she wouldn't see his smile. He didn't want to get her in trouble with his dad. But he desperately needed his phone back.

The next morning, he could hardly wait for her to leave. As he expected, she gave him his phone, but told him he could only use it for emergencies. She also asked him not to tell his father that she had given it back. Again, Jair could see the fear as she worried about the consequences.

As soon as she left, he texted Janelle.

"Sorry! Parents took phone cuz I got suspended. Can I come now?"

"My bro was mad. U gonna show this time?"

"Promise."

"K. C U soon."

He threw some clothes on. He opened the box he had hidden in a drawer and took out all his money. He counted it quickly: thirty-five and some change. He didn't know how much guns cost, but he was worried it wasn't enough. He shoved it into his jeans pocket and left to walk to Janelle's house. He turned down L Street and then onto Eighteenth. In the distance, he saw her walking ahead of him.

"Girl, you sure are fat and ugly," he said softly. He hoped no one would see him going to her house. He didn't want anyone to think he was hooking up with her.

As he got to her house, a beat-up old car pulled up to the curb. A guy got out and gave him a look. The guy was wearing a ripped gray T-shirt, jeans worn so low that his underwear showed, and a baseball cap on backward. His arms were covered with tattoos. He opened the front door and walked in, slamming it behind him.

Jair walked up to the door and knocked. Janelle opened it right away. Jair walked in and looked around. Janelle's house was more trashed than his apartment. There was a couch that had some stains on it. A coffee table was covered with McDonald's bags and a KFC tub. Empty beer bottles and cans were everywhere. The house smelled bad too, like the garbage hadn't been taken out in a while.

"Here he is," Janelle said to the guy with the tattoos. "Jair, this is Darius, my brother."

"How you doin'?" Darius said. "My sister tells me you want something."

Jair nodded. "I need a piece," he said. He hoped he sounded tough.

"How much you got?" Darius asked.

"Thirty-five. But I can get more," Jair said. "Just not right now."

Darius was laughing. "Thirty-five? Boy, that won't get you nothin'!" he said. "What you need this gun for anyway?"

Jair didn't know what Janelle had told her brother. He didn't want to tell him the truth for fear the deal wouldn't go through. "Protection," he said finally.

"Pro-tec-tion," Darius repeated. He sat quietly for a moment. "Okay, here's what I'm going to do. I'm going to lend you this piece. Long as you don't actually use it, you are just borrowing it. You use it, you've bought it, and it doesn't come back to me. I'll take your thirty-five dollars as the rental fee. If you actually use this thing, you owe me big-time. I'll come looking for you, and you'll pay what I tell you to pay. You return the piece unused, you're square with me. Understand?"

Jair nodded. He didn't want to think about what price he'd have to pay if he actually did end up using the gun. He knew Darius wasn't referring to money. He knew he'd be under Darius's control forever if he used the gun.

"Only reason I'm doing this is because Janelle asked me to," Darius said. "If you weren't her boyfriend, I wouldn't be cutting this deal. So you have her to thank," he added. "And you best treat her good, or you'll be hearing from me, got it?"

Jair didn't hear a thing after the word "boyfriend." He couldn't believe that's what Janelle had told her brother. He was trapped. If he denied being her boyfriend, he couldn't have the gun. But he didn't want to have anything to do with her. And if she told anyone at school that he was her boyfriend, he may as well drop out. No one liked Janelle. No one. Everyone just used her.

"Okay, be right back," Darius said, standing up. He walked into another room. Jair and Janelle sat without speaking. Darius came out holding a handgun. "Ever shoot one?" he asked Jair.

"Nah, but I've held one lots of times," Jair lied.

"Okay, here's what you do," Darius said. He removed the clip from the handle and then replaced it. He pointed out some of the parts of the gun and explained how it worked. Then he handed it to Jair.

Jair held it with two hands, pointing it straight ahead of him. Then he held it sideways, as he'd seen people do in movies. It was heavier than he expected, and it wobbled when he aimed it. Finally, he shoved it down the back of his pants. It scraped his skin and made it difficult to sit down.

"Be careful you don't shoot yourself in the butt," Darius said. "Now give me your cell phone. I'm going to put my number in it. You ever use this thing, you call me immediately, and I'll tell you what to do with it. I ever hear you used it and didn't call? I'll find you. Hear me?"

Jair nodded. He handed over his cell phone, and Darius put in his number.

"And, girl?" he said to Janelle, handing Jair back the phone. "Clean this place up." He walked out, slamming the screen door behind him.

Jair looked down at his feet. He had nothing to say to Janelle. He hardly even knew her. He only knew that she was the school joke—a girl that guys used for whatever they needed. Now he had used her too, just not for what she was usually used for.

"We could go in my room if you want to," she said finally.

Jair definitely did not want to. "You know I'm not your boyfriend," he said. "Why'd you tell him that?"

" 'Cause he wouldn't have helped you otherwise," she said. "But now you have to be with me because that's what you told Darius."

"I didn't tell him anything about us!" Jair said. "You did. You let him think that we were together."

"Well, you didn't say no when he said it," Janelle said. "So let's go to my room. I don't want to tell him you lied just to get the gun."

Jair felt trapped. He didn't want to have anything to do with Janelle. But he knew that with one phone call, she could get him in trouble with Darius. And Darius didn't look like someone who would tolerate someone lying about his sister to get his way.

Finally, Jair had an idea. "Okay, but not now," he said. "I have to get home before my father gets there and realizes I left. How about some other time?"

Janelle looked pleased. "My mother's never

home on weekends. How about if you come over then?"

Jair got up to leave. "Sure, whatever. Why don't you have that party you were talking about?"

"Saturday?" Janelle said.

"Yeah," Jair said. Then he had an idea. "In fact, ask that new kid, Zander, to come," he said. "Make him feel welcome." Off school property with a huge crowd around, Jair figured it was as good an opportunity as any to teach Zander a lesson. He didn't know exactly what he was going to do. He figured he would just show him the gun to scare him. Just feeling the weight of it in his waistband made him feel more powerful.

"Want to kiss me good-bye?" Janelle asked quietly, a sad, expectant look in her eyes.

"No," Jair said brutally. He walked out the door and let it slam. Somehow he had to untangle himself from the mess he'd created by taking advantage of Janelle's offer to help.

CHAPTER 12

ZANDER

For the first time in a long time, Zander looked forward to lunch. As soon as the bell rang, he hurried down to the trophy case. There were already about five or six kids there, but he had eyes for only one: Keisha. Her smile made him go warm all over.

"Hey," she said. "How'd you do on that NSL test?" she asked.

"A," he said. "How about you?"

"Bragger," she teased. "I got a B-plus. So you're smart too?"

"I do okay," he said, embarrassed. "Some classes better than others."

"But all classes better than me, I'll bet!" Ferg joked. "Don't remember the last time I got an A."

"If you studied as hard as you play, maybe that would change!" Eva said. "College is only a couple of years away, you know," she added.

"So you keep reminding me." Ferg said.

"Hey, Keisha," a voice said.

They all turned. The large girl who Zander had seen talking to Jair the day before was standing in front of the group.

"Hi, Janelle," Keisha said. "What's up?"

"I wanted to invite you to my house for a party on Saturday," the girl said. "All of you."

No one said anything for a moment. "That's really nice of you," Keisha said finally. "Thanks!"

Janelle looked at Zander. He stuck out his hand. "I'm Zander," he said. "I'm new here."

Janelle didn't shake his hand. "I know who you are," she said. "You can come too."

"Thanks," he said, putting his hand back down.

"Okay, that's it, then," Janelle said. She walked down the hall away from the group.

"What was that about?" Eva wondered.

"I have no clue," Joss answered. "But I guess there's a party Saturday night."

"What's her story?" Zander asked.

"She's kind of a sad case," Keisha said. "She needs all sorts of special classes and therapy and stuff. But she also has a really bad reputation. She goes with boys who just use her. Then they make fun of her on Facebook by posting mean comments. It's really awful. They all try to top each other with the nasty things they say about her."

"Why don't you tell them to take their posts down when they do that?" Zander asked.

"I know why *I* don't say anything—I never want to mess with those guys," Joss said. "I've read what they post, and what they do when someone disagrees with them. It's better just to ignore them."

Zander thought back to the YouTube video of the fight and how bad it made Jair look. "But it's so cruel," he said. "If enough people complained, maybe it would stop."

"Complained? How?" Ferg said. "There's no one to complain to."

"Complain to them on the site," Zander said. "Just get enough people to post the same thing, like 'Take it down,' or something like that. If a lot of people did that, wouldn't it bury what they said? Or at least make it look like people didn't want to read those things?"

Keisha had a very thoughtful look on her face. "You know, that's not a bad idea," she said finally. "I've been looking for a focus project for the school year. What if we started an anti-cyberbullying campaign that went further than what the school has now? Right now, we all know that it's bad. But what if we actually got kids to agree to take action? So if there was a post that bullied someone, everyone who saw it would respond the same way, like 'Take it down, from the Cap Central anti-cyberbullying group' or something like that. We'd have to work on the wording."

"I think it's a great idea," Joss said. "I'll help you with it."

"Me too," said Eva. "Maybe posters all over the school that read 'Take it down!' After a while, everyone will know what that expression means."

"Looks like you saved our president!" Carlos said to Zander. "Great idea, man."

The others all agreed.

"And your president thanks you," Keisha

said. "You saved my butt. I couldn't come up with any ideas. I think this is going to work. I just have to run it past Mrs. Hess."

"Well, you're on your own with that one," Zander said, shaking his head. "I want to steer clear of her! But I'm happy to help. Meanwhile, about this party Saturday ... Are you all gonna go?"

"Yeah, I'm there," Ferg said. "Anybody else?"

They all agreed they would meet at Janelle's around nine. The bell rang, and Zander joined the others walking to the third floor. He hadn't had friends for a very long time. This felt good.

CHAPTER 13

JAIR

Jair rolled out of bed. It was the day of Janelle's party. Seemed like the whole world knew about it. Facebook and Twitter were filled with people passing on messages about where the party was. From the look of things, there would be lots of alcohol. Kids were using code to say what they were planning to bring.

But Jair had bigger plans than just drinking beer. Looking in the mirror, he practiced pulling his gun out of his pants. He still hadn't come up with a plan. He mostly wanted Zander—and everyone else—to know that Jair Nobles was not someone to mess with. He wanted to look dangerous. He wanted Zander to think he was connected to dangerous people. He wanted respect.

He had fantasized all week about what he would do when he saw Zander. Make him get on his knees and beg for his life. Point the gun at him and say something cool while the guy nearly wet his pants in fear. But what to say? He'd practiced all sorts of lines, but none of them were right. He wanted to humiliate Zander, of course. But even more, he wanted everyone at the party to see him do it. He knew they had all probably watched the video of him getting beat up. They were going to understand that Zander had only caught a lucky break. Now his luck had run out. Jair hoped that he could school Zander in front of Keisha Jackson. But even if that didn't work out, he would still teach Zander a lesson.

What he hadn't decided yet was just how far he was willing to go. In his fantasies, he blasted Zander off the face of the earth. But he wasn't sure he really wanted to go that far. If he used the gun, he'd owe a huge debt to Darius Minnerly. And that wasn't something he wanted.

He also didn't know what he was going to do about Janelle. He had sort of promised he'd be with her at the party. But he actually didn't want anything to do with her. He'd gotten what he wanted from her: the gun. Let someone else take what she was offering.

He took an extra long shower and spent some time on his hair. He had to be careful what he wore. He needed a long shirt to cover the gun in his pants. When it was time to go, he felt a little sad. The thought hit him that he was taking a step from which there was no turning back.

He came out to the living room where his mom was watching TV with Marcel and Royce. "I'm going to a party," he said.

"Where is it?" his mother asked.

"Shush!" Royce said. "I'm trying to watch!"

Mrs. Nobles got up off the couch and motioned for him to come into the kitchen. "Where is it?" she asked again.

"Janelle Minnerly's house. She lives down from Cap Cent on Eighteenth Street. You remember her, she was in my fifth grade class."

He knew his mother probably wouldn't remember, but she always seemed reassured when he told her he was with someone he'd known since elementary school.

"What time will you be home?" she asked.

"Midnight?" he answered.

She nodded.

"Make sure you call me if you go anywhere else," she ordered.

"Call you how?" his father said as he walked into the kitchen. He wasn't wearing a shirt, and his pants were unbuttoned. He smelled of alcohol. Jair could see that he was drunk.

Jair realized he wasn't supposed to have his cell phone. "I'll use someone's phone," he said. He wanted to do anything he could to keep his father from getting angry at his mother.

"You could have used your own phone, except that it's not where I put it when I took it from you," his father said. "Now where do you think it is?"

Jair knew he was going to be punished. But he'd rather have his dad fight with him than with his mother. "I have it," he said. "I found it and took it back."

"Yeah? Where'd you find it?" his father asked.

Jair was trapped. He had looked all over the apartment and hadn't found the phone. His mother had given it back to him, but he didn't know where she'd found it.

"So how'd he get it back when I *know* I told you not to give it to him?" his father said to his mother.

Jair hated the frightened look in her eyes. He would do anything to help his mother. But there was nothing he could say since he didn't know where his father had hidden the phone.

"Girl, I just want to make sure I'm not misremembering this," his father said. "Didn't I tell you that he was not to have the phone?"

"Yes, but he was watching the boys, and—" his mother started.

Smack!

His father's hand slammed hard against her cheek. She gasped and held her hand to her face. Jair took a step forward, then stopped. In that moment, he hated his father more than he could ever imagine hating anyone. His father had pushed him around all his life. He was tired of it. He was tired of never doing anything right in his father's eyes. Of his father dissing him, calling him a girl. But mostly, he was tired of his father beating him and his brothers and his mother. He could feel the gun in his pants. It made him feel powerful.

"Leave her alone!" Jair shouted, stepping toward his father. "Don't you touch her."

"Jair, honey, don't!" his mother yelled. "Just leave!"

"No, Mom, I'm not leaving," Jair said. "This stops now, old man, do you hear me? No more. You don't touch her, and you don't touch the boys. It's over. Find someone else to take your misery out on, but leave us alone."

His father looked murderous. "Boy, you talking to me like that?" he said slowly.

Jair stood his ground. "I am," he said. "You can do what you want to me. You can try, anyway. You. Do. Not. Touch. Them. Again. Hear me?"

Without warning, his father charged at him. But Jair was ready. He turned away, the way he'd seen Zander do when he fought him after school. His father's momentum kept him going, and he slammed his head into the refrigerator. He sank to the floor. He looked up at Jair, dazed. "My head hurts," he mumbled.

"Listen," Jair said. "You're making a choice right now. You can stay and never touch any of us again. Or you leave. Now! But there are no other choices. What'll it be?"

His father rubbed his head and said nothing.

"I can't hear you," Jair growled. "You answer me, or I call the cops. So what's your decision?"

"I hear you," his father said. "I'll stay. And I won't hit her or them. Or you."

Jair reached down and helped his father to his feet. "And don't you think you can take this out on them when I'm not around," he said. "It's over. You ever touch anyone in this family again and I will mess you up. Got it?"

His father nodded. "I guess you think you're the man of the family now, huh?" he said. "Like you're a bigger man than me 'cause you stood up to your old dad."

"You know, I always used to respect you," Jair said. "But the man I respected wouldn't take out his anger on people who are weaker than he is. So if standing up for Mom and my brothers makes me the man of the family, then I guess that's who I am."

He turned to his mother. "You okay, Mom?"

She nodded. Her skin was still red from where his father had slapped her. But she gave him a little smile. He was glad to see that she no longer looked frightened.

"You go to your party now," she said. "We're all fine here. You just be careful, hear? If you see trouble, walk the other way."

"I will, Mom," Jair said. "I love you."

"Love you too, baby," she said.

He closed the door and stood outside for a moment. He felt a chill go up and down his spine. He wondered if he'd ever see his family again. If something happened to him, he didn't know who would protect his mother and brothers.

CHAPTER 14

ZANDER

Zander took special care getting ready for the party. He showered, even though he'd showered that morning. He stood in front of his closet and tried to figure out what to wear. He didn't want to look too L.A., but he didn't want to just throw on jeans and a T-shirt. He pulled a striped shirt out of his closet and put on his favorite jeans. It was starting to get a little cold at night, so he grabbed his leather bomber jacket and came out to the living room.

"I'm heading out," he said to his father.

"Not until we go over the rules," his father said. "Tell me what they are."

Zander sighed and sat down. "No parties where parents aren't home. No parties with alcohol or drugs. If I see trouble, I get out. If I need a ride, I call, no matter what time. I never get into a car with anyone who's been drinking or doing drugs."

His father nodded. "And my part of that rule?"

"You pick me up, no questions asked," Zander said.

"All right, son, have fun," his father said, picking up his newspaper. "I trust you. Don't betray that trust. It will be nearly impossible to get it back."

"I know," Zander said. "I'll see you later."

He knew Janelle lived near the school, so he walked that way. He hoped he could find her house, and that he would know someone when he got there. He knew that Ferg, Eva, Carlos, and Joss were going, but he didn't know exactly when they would get there. And he was very excited to see Keisha.

As he turned onto Eighteenth Street, he could hear loud music playing. He could see kids sitting on the front steps and lawn of a rundown house. He knew he was in danger of breaking one of his father's rules. He had never checked whether or not Janelle's parents would be home.

The party was already so loud that he suspected they weren't home. If they weren't, he'd leave. At least he wasn't sitting home alone on a Saturday night—for part of the night anyway.

He tried knocking at the door, but the music was too loud for anyone to hear. Soon, a group of kids he didn't recognize walked up onto the porch and opened the front door. He followed them inside.

It was even louder in the house. There were so many kids that the noise was nearly deafening. Zander looked around the living room. He saw Luther Ransome and Chance Ruffin. They were both holding red plastic cups. Luther looked up and saw Zander. He pointed Zander out to Chance. Chance said something, and they both laughed.

Zander walked toward the kitchen and saw a guy from his NSL class. The guy nodded but went on talking to the girl in front of him.

Apparently, no one he knew was there yet. As he walked back into the living room, he saw that the front door was propped open. A steady stream of kids was coming in, almost more than the house could hold. There were older people as well—guys who looked to be in their twenties. He wondered how Janelle knew them. He also wondered where she was.

He felt really awkward. He decided he needed something to do with his hands so he wouldn't look so out of place. He walked up to a girl he recognized and said, "Is there anything to drink?"

She held up a red plastic cup and yelled, "Back porch."

Zander went back into the kitchen and out the back door. There was a table set up with beer and every kind of alcohol imaginable.

Zander walked back inside. It seemed like the crowd was even larger. Something caught his eye. He looked at the stairway and saw Janelle about halfway up, trying to come down. She had a scared look on her face. Some older guys were on the stairs, not letting her pass. One of them was holding out a cell phone, probably filming. Janelle looked down at the crowd in her living room as if she were looking for help.

As Zander watched, one of the guys pushed her. She fell backward on the stairs, and the guys laughed. Then one of them stepped over her. He reached down and grabbed her under her arms. He started to pull her up the stairs while the other guys were pinching and slapping her legs. The guy with the phone went on filming.

Zander tried to push through the crowd toward the stairs. He didn't know Janelle, and his new friends had told him that she often went with guys. But this looked like she was being dragged upstairs against her will. He could hardly move due to the crush of kids in the living room.

He looked around for help and did a double-take. Jair was standing near the bottom of the stairs, facing the action in the living room. He didn't see what was happening to Janelle. He also hadn't seen Zander. Zander knew he couldn't help Janelle on his own. He needed help, and there was no one else to turn to.

"Jair!" he yelled.

Jair looked around to see who had called his name. He looked startled when he realized it was Zander. He reached his arm around to his back in a strange way.

Zander didn't have time to wonder what he was doing or to explain. He pointed up the stairs. "She needs help," Zander yelled. He continued trying to push his way to the bottom of the stairs. Jair looked up and saw a group of guys taunting Janelle as one guy pulled her up the stairs. He hesitated for a moment. Then he ran up the stairs after them.

Zander finally made it to the stairs and started up. He saw Jair near the top, but Janelle and the guys who had her were gone. Zander pushed his way through the crowd standing on the steps, shoving aside or stepping on anyone who wouldn't move.

When he reached the upstairs hallway, he saw Jair looking at three closed doors.

"I'll take this one," Jair said, opening a door.

Zander threw open the next one. Inside was a couple on the bed, making out. "Get out of here!" the guy yelled. Zander slammed the door and opened the next one.

Zander yelled, "Jair! In here!" Janelle was on the bed, and one of the guys was holding her down. The others were standing around laughing.

"Let her go. Now!" he roared. He reached for the closest guy and threw him aside. Jair burst into the room and grabbed the next guy. Zander grabbed the shirt of the guy holding Janelle down and yelled, "Get out of here! All of you!"

The guys tried pushing back a bit, but they could see it was useless. "Have fun!" one of them said as he left the room. "Didn't realize you wanted her all to yourselves!"

Janelle got up from the bed. Jair was with her, talking softly. She was crying and nodding. She straightened her clothes and left the room. The boys followed her out. As he walked down the stairs behind her, Zander could see most of the party. It was total chaos.

CHAPTER 15

JAIR

At first, Jair had thought Zander was calling him out. He heard his name, saw Zander, and reached for his piece. But something about the look on Zander's face stopped him. Something serious was going on.

He looked in the direction Zander was pointing. Immediately, he saw what was happening. Janelle was surrounded by guys who were dragging her up the stairs. No one else who cared was close enough to stop them.

Janelle was vulnerable because she was so desperate to be liked. But these weren't Cap Cent guys. They were strangers, and they were going to hurt her. Janelle wasn't going upstairs with them willingly. Whatever was going to happen next wouldn't be good.

Jair didn't like Janelle, but he also knew she needed help. And there was no one else to help her. He raced up the stairs, pushing his way through the groups of people standing around. All the bedroom doors were closed. He didn't know where the guys had taken Janelle.

He wrenched open the closest door. There was a couple arguing loudly, but the girl wasn't Janelle.

Then he heard Zander call him. He slammed the door and ran over to the bedroom where Zander was. He saw Janelle being held down on the bed.

Zander started grabbing the guys to pull them off. Jair went over to Janelle and held out his hand. She was crying. Her shirt was torn.

"You okay?" he asked her. She nodded and sat up. "This party is out of control," Jair said. "I think you'd better call your brother and ask for help." Janelle nodded and left the bedroom.

CHAPTER 16

ZANDER

Zander made his way slowly through the people standing on the stairs. All of a sudden, he heard voices yelling, "Chug! Chug! Chug!" He looked to where the chanting was coming from. He was shocked to see Keisha standing in a circle of older guys. He was surprised and disappointed that she was drinking. Then he realized that someone was holding her arms while someone else held a cup to her mouth. She tried to turn away, and the beer poured down her face.

Zander started toward her. He knew he couldn't rescue her on his own.

"Jair! Keisha, in the corner!" he yelled over his shoulder. Jair looked over to where Keisha was trapped and nodded. The two of them forced their way over to her.

When she saw them, she screamed, "Help me!"

Zander stepped in front of her just as the guy holding the cup poured the beer. It spilled down the front of Zander's shirt.

"Get her out of here!" he yelled to Jair.

"Who the hell are you?" one of the guys asked angrily.

"I'm the welterweight who's gonna pound your sorry ass if you don't let us get out of here," Zander said. "That's who." He saw Jair and Keisha making their way safely out the front door. He started backing away, keeping his eyes on the group the whole time. When he was safely away, he turned his back. It was a mistake. Someone pounded him hard between the shoulder blades. He would have gone down, but there were too many people.

He felt the old familiar rage well up inside him. He put his fists up and turned around. He looked at the guy behind him, and then at all the people in the house. If he started fighting now, it would be bedlam.

"You're not worth it, you piece of garbage," he said. He turned and walked out the front door.

CHAPTER 17

JAIR

Jair stood with Keisha at the end of the front walk. He couldn't believe how the night had turned out. When he saw the crowd at Janelle's house, he knew pulling the gun would have been crazy. Then, when he saw Janelle being attacked, he quit thinking about the gun. She didn't deserve what he suspected might be happening.

He saw the guy holding up the phone. He knew whatever they were going to do to Janelle, it would be posted online before the night was over. He knew how it hurt to have someone make a video of your humiliation and have people comment on it. Something just snapped. He didn't want what happened to him to happen to her.

First, he stood up to his father, then the guys at the party. Jair shook his head at how everything had turned out. Finally, he faced his father and demanded that he stop bullying and abusing his mother and brothers.

It would take a while for what he did to sink in. He'd gone to the party expecting to pull a gun on Zander. It was crazy that Zander ended up being the only other person who would help Janelle and Keisha. Together, the two of them took on two separate groups of older guys—and won. Without ever having to show the gun hidden in his waistband.

He was proud of himself. For the first time in his life, he had faced down some bullies. He hadn't been the bully—he'd beaten those who were bullying others. It was a good feeling. Made him feel strong. Like he was a good person. The kind of person who would risk his life to save others.

CHAPTER 18

ZANDER

Zander left Janelle's house and saw Jair and Keisha waiting for him on the sidewalk. He held out his hand to Jair. "We did good in there, homes," he said.

Jair hesitated for a moment. Then he took Zander's hand and shook it. "Don't know what's gonna happen to Janelle now," he said. "But that was ugly."

"Janelle?" Keisha asked. "What happened to Janelle?"

Zander told her how Jair had charged up the stairs when they had seen that Janelle was in trouble. He described the mob scene on the stairs, and how they'd burst into the bedroom where Janelle was being held down.

"So you guys rescued Janelle *and* me? What

heroes!" Keisha said. "Seriously, that was the most scared I've ever been. If you guys hadn't come, I don't know what I would have done. You were both so brave."

Jair shrugged. "You know, we should probably get out of here," he suggested. "I'll bet the cops will be here soon. All these neighbors? Just a question of time. We need to be gone. I don't want them to question us."

Zander wiped his hands down the front of his shirt. "I'm soaked in beer," he said. "My dad's going to think I was drinking—I smell."

"That might be me," Jair said with a laugh.

"Or me," Keisha said. "Face it, we all stink."

They walked down to K Street and turned the corner onto Seventeenth.

"You Cap Cent kids really know how to throw a party." Zander laughed. "And here I thought living in Washington, D.C., would be boring! Who were all those people anyway? A lot of them didn't look like they were even our age."

"I have no idea," Keisha replied. "I've never seen most of them before. They're not Cap Cent kids."

"Someone posted something on Facebook about the party. The texts were flying. Word spread," Jair said. "There are probably kids here from all over D.C., Maryland, and Virginia."

"I hate to sound naive," Zander said, "but does she have parents? My father would kill me if I ever had a party like that."

"She's got a mom, but I don't think she was home," Keisha said. "Parties like these don't happen when parents are around."

"Have you been to other parties like this?" Zander asked. "Whoa, that sounded like I was judging you. I was actually just curious. I've never seen anything like this."

"Actually, I stay away," Keisha said. "These parties always get raided by the cops. Even though I don't drink, if I got caught at a party where alcohol was served, I'd have to resign as SGA president. So I'm really careful."

Behind them, they could hear cars tearing up the street with their brakes squealing. Someone threw a bottle. "This is going to get ugly," Zander said, turning toward the sound.

Keisha pulled out her phone. "I want to text

Joss and Eva to tell them not to show up. Do you guys want to come to my house? I can tell them to meet us there, and we can hang out."

"Sounds good," Zander said. "We need to keep away everyone we can."

Keisha turned to Jair. "Jair?" she asked. "Would you like to come over?"

"I should probably go," Jair said. "I've got to work on my story for my parents as to why I smell like this."

"That's going to be a problem for me too," Zander added. "Hey, Jair, I have an idea … not about the smell, but … I don't know if you're interested. Mr. Gable, the security guard, runs a group in the weight room at the school," he said. "I checked it out a few days ago. It has speed bags, punching bags, weights. Everything. I'm going to start going after school. Do you want to check it out?"

Jair thought it sounded great. He had to admit, he wished he knew as much as Zander did about fighting. Watching Zander face off against the guys messing with Janelle and Keisha made Jair think that learning some boxing moves might be the way to go. But he didn't know the first thing about fighting, and he didn't want to look foolish.

"Nah, no need," he said. Then he stopped. "Truth be told, I don't know how to use that stuff," Jair said.

"I'm sure he'd help you," Zander said. "Up to you, man. Tuesdays, Wednesdays, and Thursdays. If you want to check it out, meet me there."

Jair nodded. "Later," he said as he turned to walk down the street.

"Wait! Jair?" Keisha said.

He stopped and waited as she walked over to him.

"Thanks," she said. "You're the best." She kissed him on the cheek.

Jair felt warm all over.

"Aw, shucks," he said, blushing. "It weren't nothin'."

"Was to me," she said. "I won't forget it."

Zander held out his hand again. "Later," he said.

Jair shook his hand. "See ya, homes," he said as he headed up the street.

CHAPTER 19

JAIR

Jair started walking toward his apartment. He was so happy that Keisha had invited him over. For a moment, he considered it. But then he pictured himself sitting with Keisha and her friends, and he knew he wouldn't be comfortable. He'd be okay with Zander, surprisingly, but there was too much nasty history with her other friends. They had never liked him, so he had never liked them.

But there was another reason too. Jair could see what he'd been hiding from himself for the past few days. Keisha had eyes only for Zander. There was no sense fooling himself. He didn't have a chance with her. But being her friend was the next best thing.

Meanwhile, there was something he had to do. He dialed a number on his phone.

"Darius?" he said. "I need to meet with you, man. I have something of yours I want to return."

CHAPTER 20

ZANDER

Zander and Keisha walked to her block. "Well, that was interesting," Zander said. "Who would have thought that Jair and me would be on the same side."

"Thank goodness you were," Keisha said. "You guys were superheroes, saving all us damsels in distress."

"Is that how you see yourself?" Zander said. "Because you seem like a girl who can take care of herself."

"Maybe, but I still have to face my parents," Keisha said. "I have no idea what I'm going to tell them about why I smell like beer."

"I always find that telling the truth is easier in the long run," Zander offered. "Makes it easier to answer questions. And you didn't do anything wrong, except maybe going in the first place."

"Well, I also have to answer to Mrs. Hess," Keisha said. "I have to tell her that I was at the party in case someone tells her that they saw me. I'm relieved none of my other friends were there. Everyone at that party can be kicked out of any clubs and teams that they're on. I saw Luther Ransome and Chance Ruffin, a couple of our football players. It's strange, though. The two of them never seem to get caught doing the stuff everyone knows they do. Meanwhile, you, Jair, and I can vouch for each other, backing each other up about how we tried to leave when we figured out what kind of a party it was."

Zander looked at his watch. "Okay, it's nine twenty. So that's our story? We left about ten minutes ago. I'll back you and you back me, okay? Meanwhile, I don't much care about Mrs. Hess. I broke almost every rule my father has. He's the one I'm worried about. Even though it wasn't my fault."

"No, but you'd better have a good story when you see him," Keisha said, laughing. "As someone with brothers, I can tell you that 'it wasn't my fault' rarely works."

They continued walking down the street. Zander loved that she was still holding his arm. They were so close he could smell the strawberry-scented shampoo she used. All of a sudden, he had a terrible thought. He wondered if she was so comfortable holding his arm and walking with him because she still thought he was gay.

He stopped walking. He had to set the record straight. He knew it was risky. She might be uncomfortable to know he actually liked girls. But it had to be said.

"Hey, Keisha, there's something I've been meaning to tell you," Zander said.

Keisha looked up at him and stepped closer. "Yes?"

He could feel her breath on his face. He closed his eyes for a moment. "I'm not gay," he confessed.

Keisha smiled. Her whole face lit up. She put her arms around him and kissed him softly.

"I know," she said.

ABOUT THE AUTHOR

Leslie McGill was raised in Pittsburgh. She attended Westminster College in New Wilmington, Pennsylvania, and American University in Washington, D.C. She lives in Silver Spring, Maryland, a suburb of Washington, D.C., where she works in a middle school library. She lives with her husband, a newspaper editor, and has two adult children, both of whom have chosen to live as far from home as possible.